Art & Soul...
Creative journaling from the inside out

Sylvia D. Miller, author and illustrator

Copyright 2017 by Sylvia D. Miller

No part of this book may be reproduced, stored in a retrieval system or transmitted in any form or by any means, electronic, mechanical, photocopying, recording or otherwise, without express written permission of the publisher, except for brief quotations or critical reviews.

ISBN #978-0-9983677-2-9
Library of Congress Control Number: 2017932526

Published by:
Applegate Valley Publishing
411 Greentree Loop
Grants Pass, OR 97527

www.sylviamillerwatercolor.com
www.applegatevalleypublishing.com

Cover and interior design by Deborah Perdue, Illumination Graphics
www.illuminationgraphics.com

PRINTED IN U.S.A.

Dedication

*I dedicate this book,
Art and Soul,
to my two dear sisters,
Barbara J. Roberts and
Vicky S. Galberth*

Introduction

"This is my time to live. I am awed by life itself. It is a new energy."

I had no idea that these strokes of ink on a blank page were the beginning of a subtle tsunami. I left my first marriage of thirty plus years. We had tried so hard to be nice to each other, to not offend or hurt the other's feelings, that we forgot to allow the other person space to grow. My next relationship was more open; in an understanding and in a kind way, I could grow. This began my awareness into what life is and my purpose for being. Little by little, my inner vision opened. The fleeting moments of consciousness grew, like compound interest, into a new collective perspective. Now, I stood in awe, gazing out over a broader horizon of my life.

In 2005, I sought answers to this ever-extending field of vision. I visited the Center for Spiritual Living in Grants Pass, Oregon. Here, I felt I would be able to find the answers to the questions about my growing perspective. I moved, and upon completing an intensive 4-year program, I became a Certified Licensed Practitioner of Science of Mind in 2015 at the New Thought Center for Spiritual Living in Lake Oswego, Oregon. Like clay molded into form, my life as a child had been punched and pushed in many directions before it solidified into its self-assured state. I came to realize that the knowledge of Truth would set me free, and the conditions, circumstances and ills of yesterday would disappear. I learned that I was supported and comforted by a loving, sustainable God. A forgiving heart provided freedom from my own self-imposed bondage. Life is innately good, I believe, and if I persisted in seeing good, then that which is good would triumph. Life had been good all along, I think, but I had not quite recognized it.

Everyone's nature is spiritual. It is of God. This is our changeless reality. Negative experiences may seem to exist for a brief moment, but Truth and Love exist forever. This knowing is what I had sought. During the years of practitioner's studies, I memorized over and over again a line that became the motto that would guide my life. "I surrender to the power and presence of God within." No longer was I disturbed by the passage of time, or the idea of aging or feeling stuck, waiting at a stop sign. My thoughts and I became one with the universe, one with God. Life is filled with joy when we believe that God is the Power and the Presence that is in behind everything. God is perfect and ever giving. God is love.

Every time I open my sketchbook to draw or write, I center in on that inner essence. It is a meditative, inspirational and creative process. My journal is where I express my life. Often, feelings stuck deep in my guts are released by my work on the page. It is a spiritual, heartfelt sense that calls from the caverns of my being. When I listen, it is as if I allow everything in my life to begin anew. Within this new consciousness, I am wide-awake with new ideas. The more I allow it, the more this newness bears fruit, in accordance to the divine pattern.

As long as I can remember, I have drawn. Since my college days, I have filled countless numbers of sketchbooks with drawings. I have always had a desire to express my heart's voice on the sketchbook page. In the process of filling countless journals, I have discovered, I am a writer. Creative spiritual journaling is a place where I work out my frustrations. Gratitude lists, new ideas and records of wonderful moments allow me to vent anger and handle problems larger than life. It is a safe place to fully experience myself. It is a private place to be shared or not. With growing regularity, the pages in my sketchbooks kept turning over, like leaves on a one-hundred-year old oak. Eventually, my drawings and writings evolved to where one inspired the other. The writing of Ernest Holmes, Sunday services at the Centers for Spiritual Living, travels, workshops, books I read, old newspaper clippings, family photos, memories, random notes from years gone, and sitting meditatively in my favorite corner chair with my morning coffee – all were triggers to the creative process.

Life continues to unfold, but the transitions seem smoother. I have established a spiritual bank account from which to draw; it's my security and comfort in time of need. My new awareness of that inner strength and support would show me how to be successful and prosper, how to be happy and content. I know that I am in a partnership with the Infinite and failure is impossible.

Within the pages of my journals and sketchbooks, I have chronicled my personal understanding about life. When obstacles get in the way, the spaces on the page reveal insights on how to handle them. The principles of truth continue to strengthen and support my life. I am the master craftsman in charge of creating a life of choice that is free from any unwanted past conditions or beliefs. I choose to grow as a person who is true to the consciousness of my own Self. I have surrendered to the power and presence of Spirit within. That is where the answers to all of my questions are found. This is my faith.

As we walk our path of truth, and live the expression of who we are, we learn to see more clearly, from the inside out. By paying attention to ourselves, we are able to feel, hear and see the way for any particular project or plan we might have. "There is nothing you cannot do, if you can imagine it."

My purpose is one of being in loving service to the Universe. I graciously share Spirit's special gifts that flow through me, with you. I lovingly bare my heart and soul completely… from the inside out.

Sylvia D. Miller
Certified Licensed Spiritual Practitioner
Lake Oswego, Oregon

Table of Contents

Bonsai and Baby Dolls	2
Coins and Cronies	4
Atascadero Creek	6
White Laundry	8
10,000 Lights	10
Ravaged Souls	12
Masks	14
Turn the Key	16
A Gift of Grief	18
Amongst Divinity	20
How Stories Get Started	22
The Clockworks Turn	24
Enjoy the View	26
Ladies Only	28
Yellow Truck Wisdom	30
The Company of Mice	32
China Experience	34
Turning Point	36
Time to Move On	38
Chew On Coca	40
The Man in the Doorway	42
Morning Coffee	44
Morning Mantras	46
Wholeness	48
Breasts are Beautiful	50
The Brick Wall	52
The Dimmer Switch	55
Make Me an Instrument	56
Surrender	58
The Eye of the Storm	60
Primordial Soup	62
Original Brew	64
Monkey Matters	66
Love that Sticks	68
Paper Dolls	70
Red Dance Shoes	72
Next O'Kin	74
Basic Foundation	76
Fall into Freedom	78
Love Beyond Boundaries	80
Team Rowing	82
A Little Bit of Heaven	84
Pearls of Wisdom	86
Folded Cranes	88
Black Dots	90
Indwelling Spirit	92
One God, Many Paths	94
Learning Patience	96
Varanasi Gnats	98
Miracles	100

Bonsai and Baby Dolls

Old newspaper clippings stir up emotions and criticisms. They release prejudices and guilt. These memories are of my sister's horrible fate. She lived four months after the wood stove fire. More than a hundred people, mostly strangers, volunteered skin for the massive grafting procedures that were necessary to try and save her life. She became a tabloid celebrity. I grew jealous of all her attention. I felt frightened and alone. How dare she leave me.

Very few gave us siblings much regard. My third grade teacher gave me a baby doll to love and hold. I sought solace in the neighbor's bonsai garden. Finally, I had a friend. He glued pieces of cloth together and made clothes for my doll. My mother's reaction was that I should not play across the street because the family was Japanese. Silently, I slipped into a long period of lapsed memory. I have never been able to retrieve what was forgotten.

I forgive. I am forgiven. All past is now wiped out of my consciousness. I am free of oppression and guilt. I am grateful for baby dolls and bonsai trees.

"There isn't any memory, no matter how intense that doesn't fade out at last."
—Juan Rulfo

Coins and Cronies

"No matter what our emotional storm, or what our objective situation may be, there is always something hidden in the inner being that is never violated."
—Ernest Holmes

I was not aware that my sister, too, had fallen prey to his tricks and threats. Our happiness was not destroyed by the negative experiences we had gone through, but by the feelings and emotions carried from our childhood memories. Eventually, sisters talk to each other.

The greatest gift we can give ourselves is to know the truth, our truth. The truth negates the judgments we carried for so long. We were never bad or wrong. We tried to take care of ourselves. We tried to survive the best way we knew how.

There was a crony who jingled coins in his pocket for little girls to reach in and grasp. Knowing we could not swim, he would threaten to throw us into a deep swimming hole if we told anyone about what we would touch in his pockets. This is what caused our loss of self-respect. To be gentle with ourselves and to let go of judgment is to give ourselves the truth of who we are.

Atascadero Creek

"Often I listen to it. Often I look into it eyes, and always I have learned from it. Much can be learned from a river."
— "Siddhartha" by Herman Hesse

We felt a deep love for the seasonal creek. Its mystery is that it is in all places at once; at its source, on its way to the Russian River, to its mouth at Jenner by the Sea in Northern California. Hidden from us kids, the Atascadero Creek started somewhere in the nearby coastal foothills.

It flowed northward. Its winter floods covered miles of barb wired fencing, forsaking herds of cattle. As a late spring brook, its trickles snaked around emerald green islands where our imaginations owned their own kingdoms and the water irrigated brewery hop. In the summer, it starved into dry-locked swimming holes where my brothers could catch fish with their bare hands. In Fall, the turtles and toads buried themselves under chocolate pudding-like, leftover mud.

There is not past, present or future of the water. Creeks grow into rivers. There are no secrets.

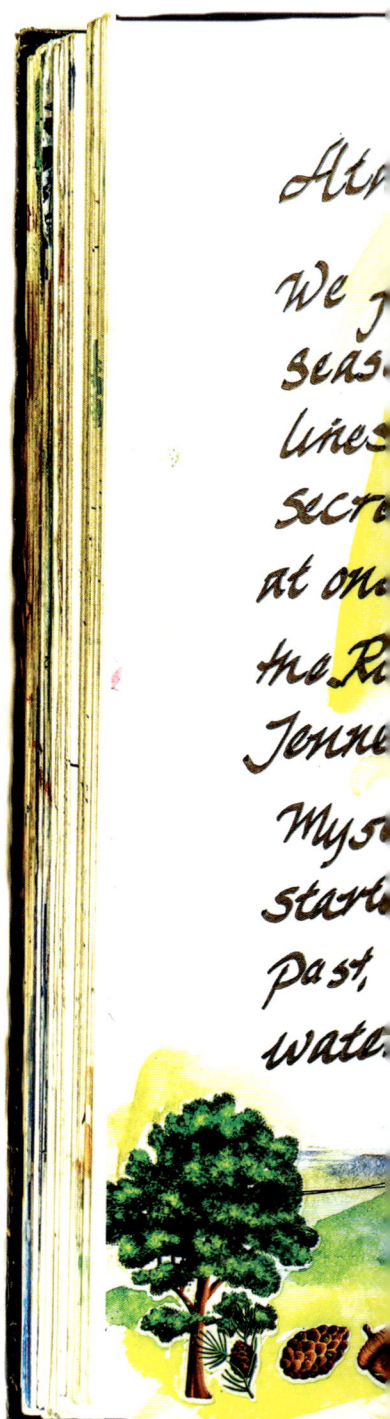

Creek

deep love for the
eek; the irredescent
movement, so rich its
a creek is all places
source, on its way to
River, its mouth at
he sea in California.
, to us kids the creek
ewhere. There is no
t or future of the
are no shadows.

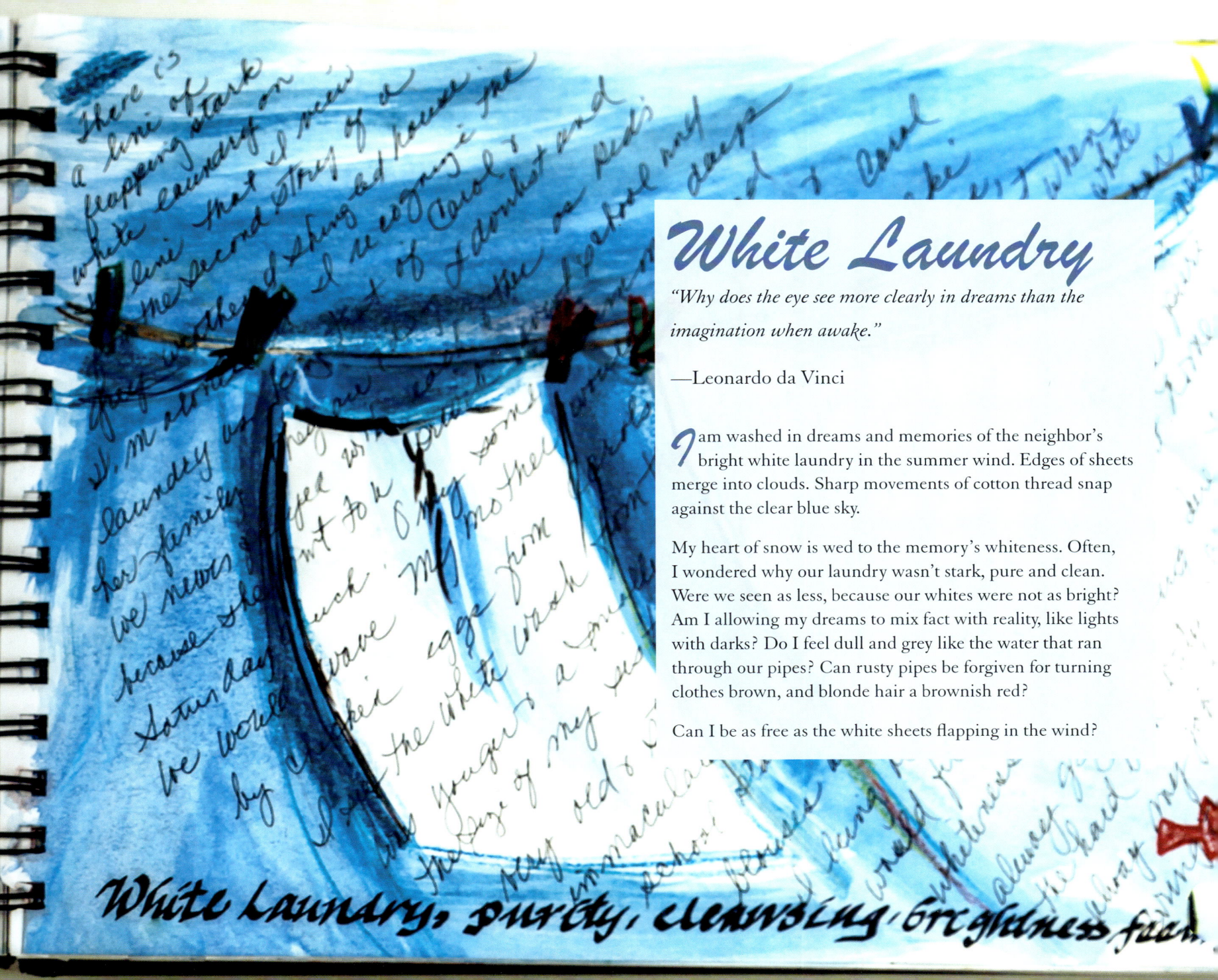

White Laundry

"Why does the eye see more clearly in dreams than the imagination when awake."

—Leonardo da Vinci

I am washed in dreams and memories of the neighbor's bright white laundry in the summer wind. Edges of sheets merge into clouds. Sharp movements of cotton thread snap against the clear blue sky.

My heart of snow is wed to the memory's whiteness. Often, I wondered why our laundry wasn't stark, pure and clean. Were we seen as less, because our whites were not as bright? Am I allowing my dreams to mix fact with reality, like lights with darks? Do I feel dull and grey like the water that ran through our pipes? Can rusty pipes be forgiven for turning clothes brown, and blonde hair a brownish red?

Can I be as free as the white sheets flapping in the wind?

10,000 Lights

The Tao is another word for Self, which projects itself into everything. Great teachers point the way, so students can see through life into their own self, to see their own unlimited potential possibilities. Like clay molded into form, my life as a child was punched and pushed in many directions before it came into its final self-assured state of being. Teachers touch my soul, my-Self, my worth.

My heart began to sing. I learned to forgive and to forget. I moved into a space of love, full circle love. I became a teacher. To this day, I receive telephone calls from former students who let me know I made a difference in their lives. On one occasion, there was 35 years between our last contact. Time melted into nothingness. Our love connection was timeless.

Teachers allow each person's light to shine. Out of each, emerges 10,000 lights that shine.

"The bible states, "In the beginning there was the word." The Buddha states, "In the beginning there was reasoning." And the Tao states, In the beginning there is the Tao."

Dr. Reverend Ruth Miller

Boxed Burdens

"Maybe she's pregnant," one girl whispered. "I heard she ran away," declared another. I pretended that I didn't know our classmate in question. She was a victim of rape. I knew the truth. She was only 14 years old. Only a person who has experienced such deep trauma really understands. `

Do I speak up or do I "go along to get-along?" I kept the burden of silent tears buried, deeply hidden in an undisclosed place, like at the back of a garden where nothing grows. Finally, God's love would reveal the consuming confidences in my mind which were released by my new found strength in Spirit.

Theodore Roosevelt wrote, "In our ignorance we misuse our divinity without destroying it. Society holds us back." When we stay silent because we don't want to be judged by our peers or society, we are hiding the divine spark within us, contributing to our own bondage.

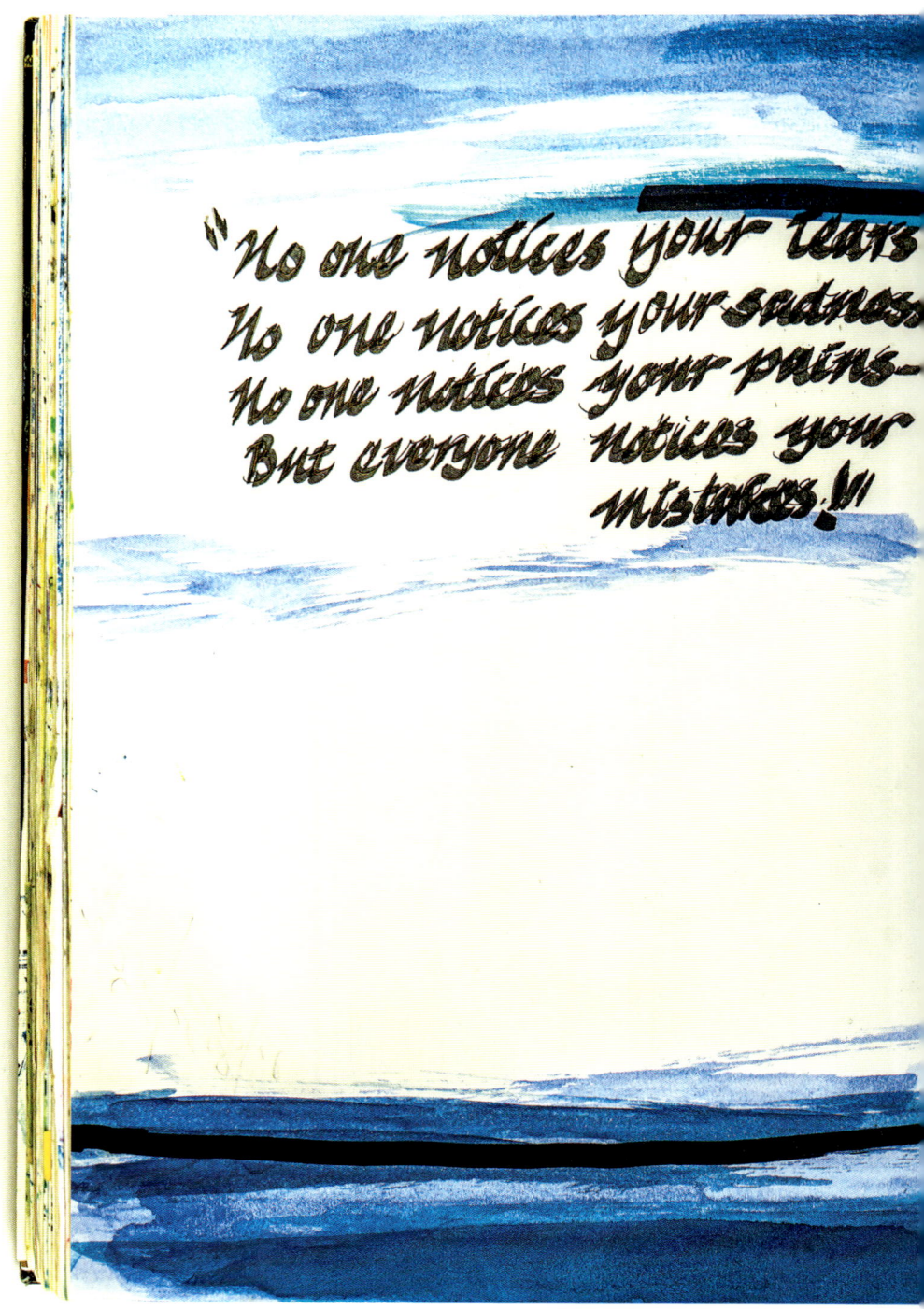

"No one notices your tears
No one notices your sadness
No one notices your pains—
But everyone notices your mistakes!"

"I just want to sleep, a coma would be nice, or amnesia. Anything, just get rid of this, these thoughts, whispers in my mind. Did he rape my mind, too?"

—Laurie Halse Anderson

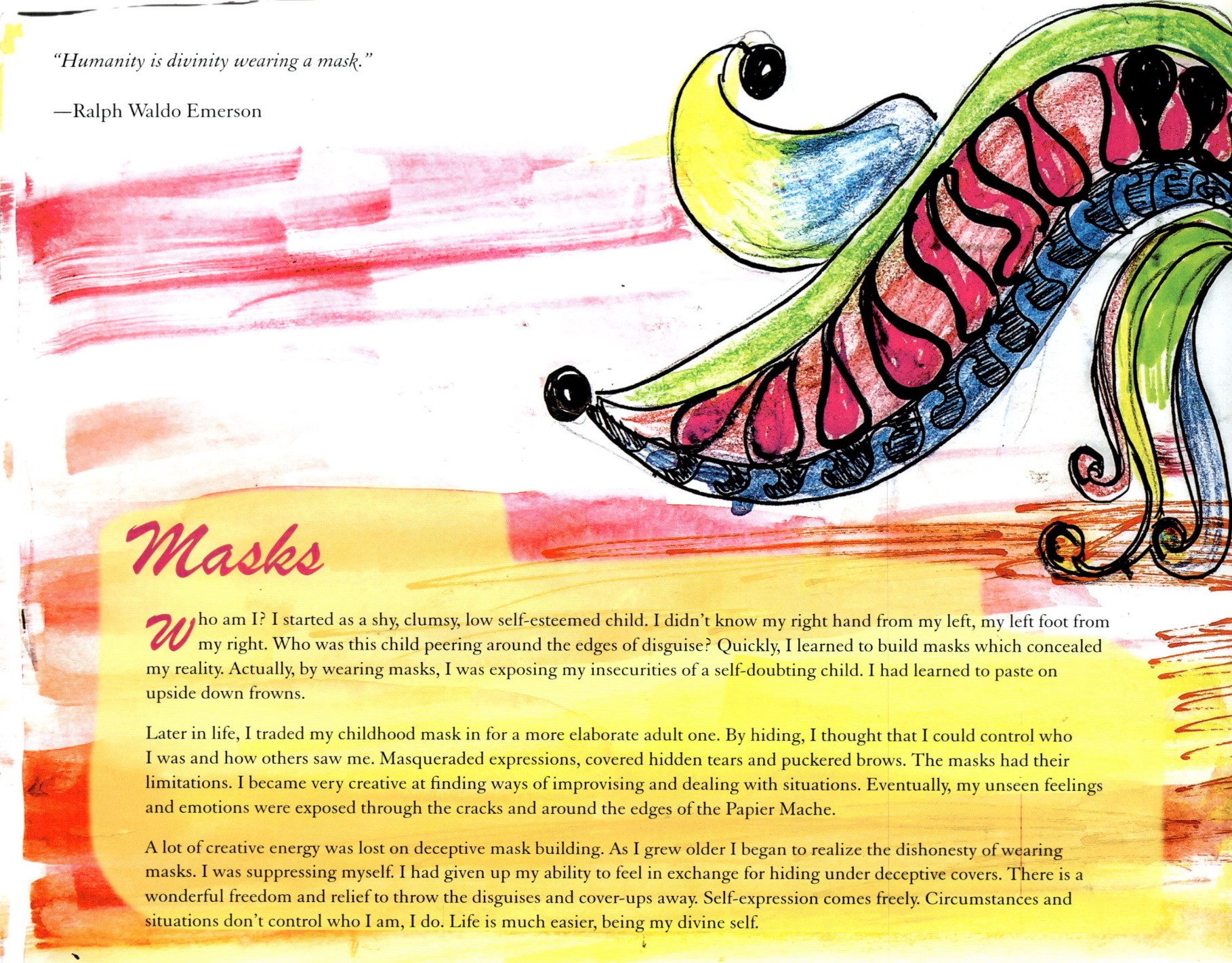

"Humanity is divinity wearing a mask."

—Ralph Waldo Emerson

Masks

Who am I? I started as a shy, clumsy, low self-esteemed child. I didn't know my right hand from my left, my left foot from my right. Who was this child peering around the edges of disguise? Quickly, I learned to build masks which concealed my reality. Actually, by wearing masks, I was exposing my insecurities of a self-doubting child. I had learned to paste on upside down frowns.

Later in life, I traded my childhood mask in for a more elaborate adult one. By hiding, I thought that I could control who I was and how others saw me. Masqueraded expressions, covered hidden tears and puckered brows. The masks had their limitations. I became very creative at finding ways of improvising and dealing with situations. Eventually, my unseen feelings and emotions were exposed through the cracks and around the edges of the Papier Mache.

A lot of creative energy was lost on deceptive mask building. As I grew older I began to realize the dishonesty of wearing masks. I was suppressing myself. I had given up my ability to feel in exchange for hiding under deceptive covers. There is a wonderful freedom and relief to throw the disguises and cover-ups away. Self-expression comes freely. Circumstances and situations don't control who I am, I do. Life is much easier, being my divine self.

Use the Key

From my mother's pocket came a set of beloved keys— keys that had opened and shut childhood recollections and memories. Keys to front doors gone by, curio closets, outmoded cars and a timeworn cedar chest. They were the keys to my heart.

4/19/2016

Turn the Key

"The key of persistence opens all doors closed by resistance."
— John Di Lemme

She pulled her beloved keys out of her pocket. Keys from front doors gone by, keys that open strange closets, keys which ignited old cars that now sit as piles of rust. My childhood memories, some that were shut and some that were open, were handed to me by my mother as her final, dying gift.

The key collection grew as my recollections of life were nurtured. I would acquire additional keys that would continue to provide me comfort and protection.

All of the answers to life's key questions lie deep within the silent pockets of my heart. Only Spirit can hold the keys which open or lock our heart's answers. Take the key, Spirit. Take all of my keys. Break the lock of my heart with this key of hope. Deeply, diligently, I feel my way into the pockets.

The Gift of Grief

*"A flower bloomed early, already wilted.
Beginning its life with an early ending."*
— R.J. Gonsales

I didn't know how to manage these unfamiliar emotions surrounding the loss. No one gets to tell you how to feel except yourself. I thought by burying them they would disappear and eventually, I would heal. Also, I realized that at the age of forty the opportunity of another pregnancy was unlikely.

There were elements of depression that need to be addressed, but at the time I or no one around me suggested that I get help. Yet, at other times when I found life disappointing, I had something to hold on to. I saw it as a gift. I never lost sight I had been granted the pregnancy in the first place. I have always carried that with me, like a priceless gift…the sight of that luminous package.

Amongst Divinity

"Nothing is more indispensable to true religiosity than a mediator that links us to divinity."

— Novalis

Amongst our group of travelers is a single gentleman, a delightful, humorous conversationalist. There is constant competition between the ladies of the group for this bachelor's attention.

We are on a day excursion to Hozoviotissa Monastery on the Cycladic Island of Amorgos. It is a beautiful blend of nature's reality and man's creation. I sensed the divinity of the place the moment I set foot on this holy ground.

We climb a thousand steps straight up the side of the vertical whitewashed walls. Mismatched windows provide magnificent views of the sparkling blue waters of the Aegean Sea, 3,000 meters below. Inside, the thick and cool ancient walls greet us with portraits of monks, smells of incense, icons and other small treasures. The monks, who act as guardians of this architectural marvel, serve us raki (a local liqueur) and loukomi.

Immediately, the bachelor and the monk strike up an intense conversation about history and religion. Slowly, it is revealed that our gentleman is an eminent Roman Catholic priest.

A Greek orthodox monk, a Roman Catholic priest on a holiday, and a small group of painters commune together. It leaves a lasting impression on my mind of the Oneness of everything, a unique feeling hard to explain in words; a spiritual awakening, beyond comprehension.

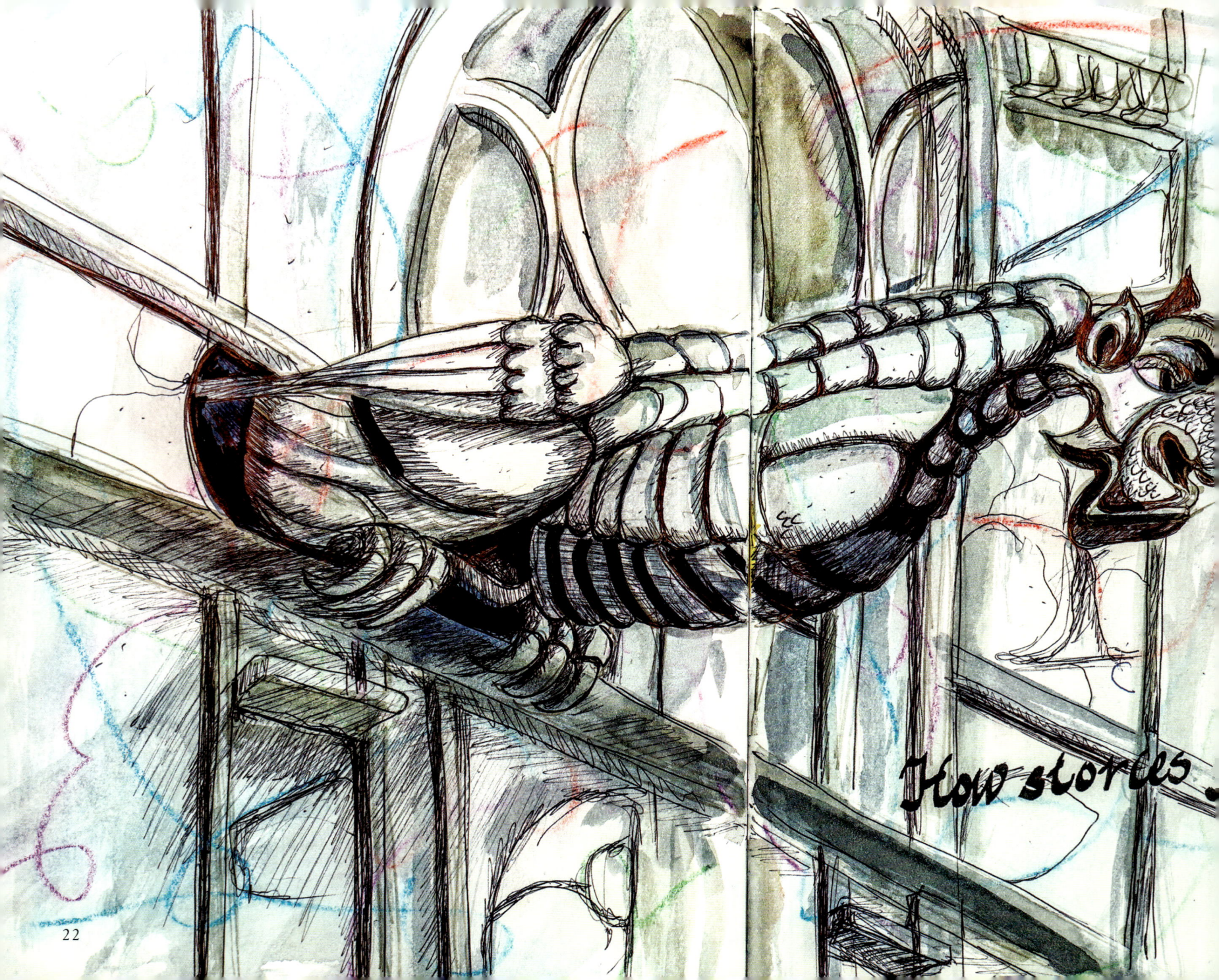

How Stories Get Started

Twisted supernatural beings, gargoyles, sit perched on edges of ancient buildings in the city of Hong Kong. They remind the faithful of the evils from which the church protects. It was Good Friday, 4 o'clock on the dot. Thunder and lightning tore open the skies.

Rain pelted the high vaulted ceilings with such force, I felt the stone walls of the cathedral tremble. As the service commenced, Beth and I sat in a pew, mesmerized. High above, through the stain glass windows, I watched torrential rain empty the heavens. It gushed down and poured out the wide open mouths of the grotesque stone figures, onto the ancient cobblestones below. In the aftermath, we waded through a foot of water.

The mere vision of gargoyles is capable of filling the likes of me with fear and revulsion. I adore these fanciful clown-like images. Experiencing the rain so vividly added powerful theatrical touches to our Hong Kong drama. It is easy to see how stories of old, legends and teachings get started.

"Fearsome creatures who would stay.
Unchanged by the light of day.
Remain you thus throughout the night.
Be thou flesh by dawn's fair light."

—William Shakespeare, "
   A Mid-Summers Night's Dream"

SYLVIA

The never ending cycle of time~
5/30/2013

The Clockworks Turn

"The whole history of science has been the realization that events do not happen in an arbitrary manner, but rather that they reflect a certain underlying order which may or may not be divinely inspired."

—Stephen Hawking

We had brought everything needed for a six-month painting sabbatical. After a 13-hour journey, it took every ounce of energy to haul ourselves on top of the twin beds. We fell into a deep sleep.

The next morning, we were woken by buoyant laughter, blasting horns, banging doors and running showers. The light of dawn illuminated our apartment. Brewed coffee brought us to life. Exploring the city was foremost on our mind. We had neglected to change our watches. I took the elevator down to the front desk to check on the time. The "light of dawn" streaming into our apartment was the illumination of the night's street lights. It was 2:00 AM, Madrid time!

Time is an arbitrary creation dictated by human needs and lifestyles. Daytime and nighttime at one place is nighttime and daytime at another. It is a beautifully inspired never ending cycle. The clockworks turn and man gives the phenomenon a name. The name of the form is time.

"Enjoy the View"

> "Life is like a ten speed. Most of us have gears we have never used."
> —Charles Schultz

Climb a hill. Coast down. Climb, crest, coat. Westerly fingers of fog drift over the coastal ranges spilling into the foothills and valleys of Sonoma County. Bursts of emerging sunshine awaken spring sunrise. The scent of white lilies and blue lupine mix. Fragrant fresh sea air finds its way to the sense of smell. Giant old oaks open their wounded wombs to honey sweetness. Newborn lambs are bleating.

My legs aren't aware of their fatigue. Incredulously, I am overwhelmed by it all. I keep peddling. The magical landscape is forever changing. Life is much like riding a bike. If you stop peddling, you fall over. If you are to enjoy life and reap the benefits, you must keep each foot strapped to the peddles. Gear down. Allow the ratcheting chain to continue cultivating the lifecycle. Keep peddling to enjoy the view.

Susan B. Anthony wrote, "She who succeeds in gaining mastery of the bicycle will gain the mastery of life."

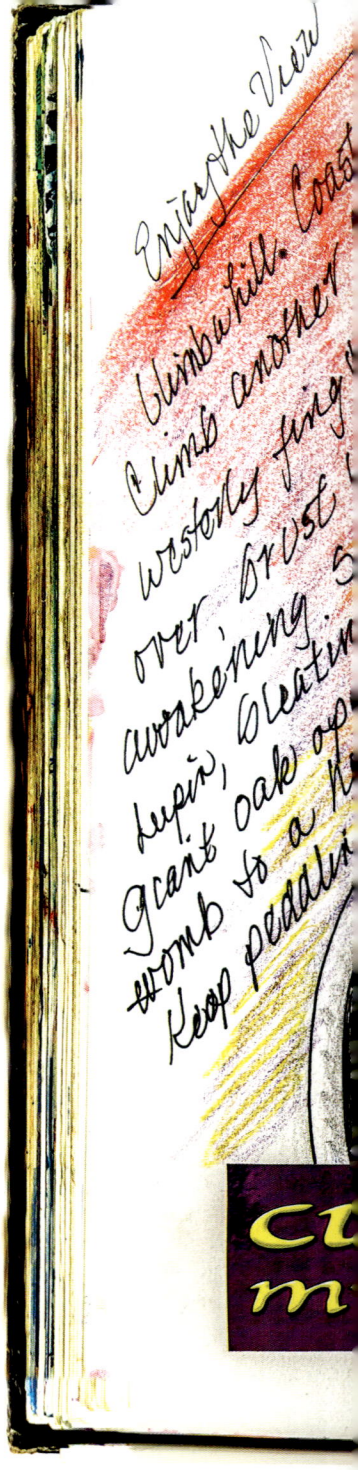

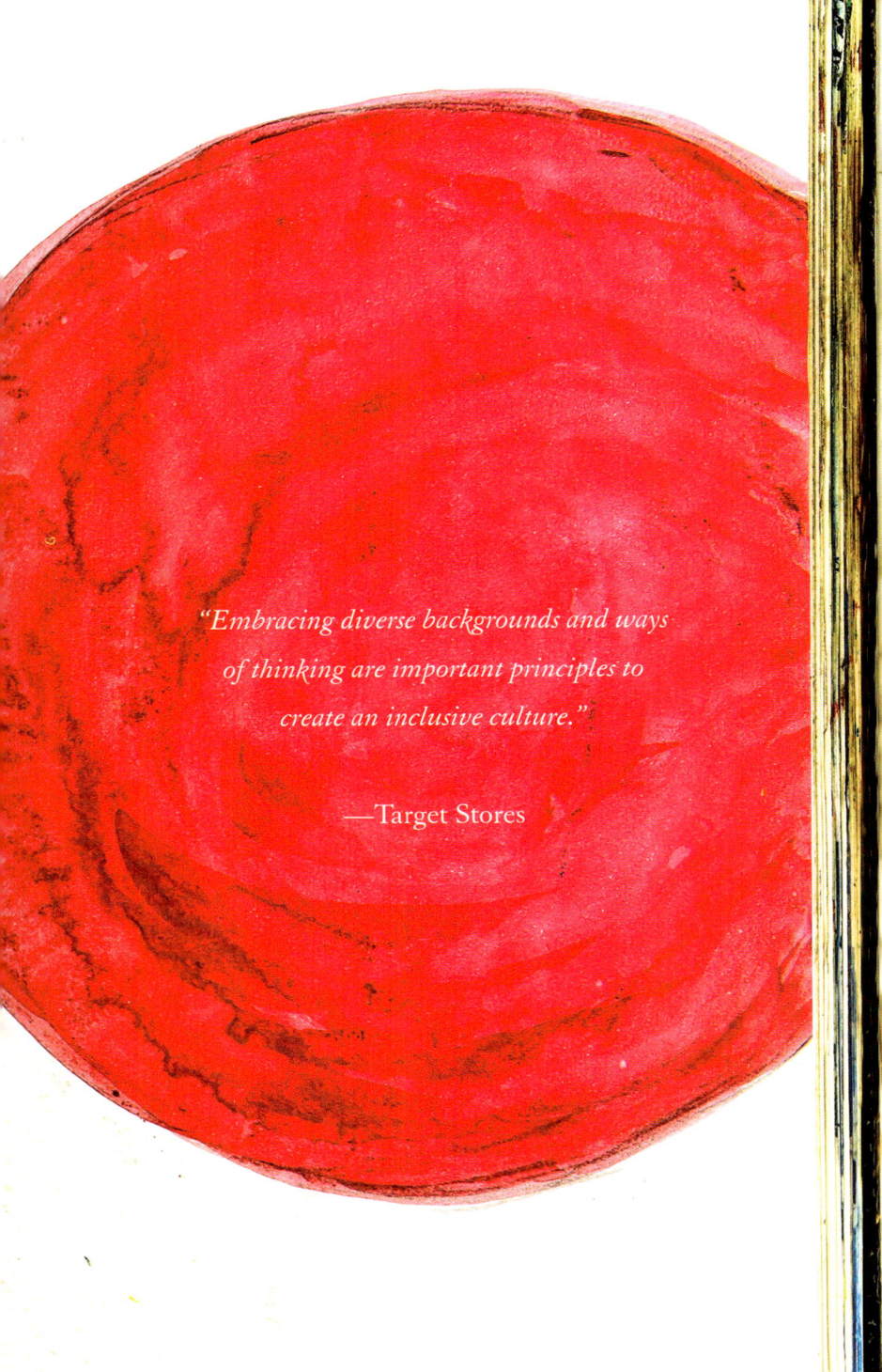

"Embracing diverse backgrounds and ways of thinking are important principles to create an inclusive culture."

—Target Stores

Ladies Only

I was trying on clothes at Macy's in the privacy of my cubicle. To use the three way mirrors, I stepped out of my private dressing room. Another well attired lady was doing the same thing. We carried on a lengthy conversation. Do you like this color on me? Does this really make me look a full size smaller like the label says?

We laughed together. After the encounter, I thought what a charming person that was. Her lovely deep voice gave her identity away. Did I feel uncomfortable, insecure or embarrassed? Hell no! Are you ready for something else? This diary entry was made 30 years ago!

Transgender people have been using the same dressing rooms all along. Agreeing and disagreeing, is your choice. Everyone deserves to feel like they belong, to feel accepted, welcomed and respected. When Target takes a stand for inclusivity, they celebrate a world that works for everyone.

Yellow Truck Wisdom

Are you listening for the rain? At the age of 96, our fond, old friend George was still working at Imwalli's Gardens. He delivered farm fresh produce to the local Italian restaurants in his worn yellow pick up. His truck always sat on the street in front of his house on A Street.

One day, we caught a glimpse of George sitting in his truck, windows reflecting streaks of white and yellow rain. Later, George remained in his truck. Then later and later. Worried, I knocked on the truck window. He didn't answer the knock, or the next or next.

Anxiously, thinking the very worst, I jerked on the door's handle. Startled, he opened his eyes. I shouted, "Are you okay?" George said, "I can no longer hear the rain inside my home, so I come out here to sit so I can listen to the raindrops hit the roof top."

"It requires wisdom to understand wisdom. The music is nothing if the audience is deaf."

—Walter Lippman

In the Company of Mice

"Be not afraid, only believe."

—Mark 5:36

In the company of mice

She said I could smell the coffee from Mark West Springs Road. I stopped by on my way to work to see what was happening on the ranch. Also, it was to check on her. In her late 80s, Winnie raised a farm menagerie. Her favorites were topped-notched Bantams with fluffy feathered feet. She called each one by name. She would latch down the chicken house at sundown to keep out the marauding raccoons and bobcats.

One morning Winnie was not in the house. I found her in the chicken pen. Unfortunately, she had fallen there the night before. I felt awful that she had to lie on the ground all night. After she returned from the hospital, I asked her about that night. She said, "I had chicken feed in my hands. While I laid on the ground, little mice came and went. They ate grain out of my palm. I could feel their whiskers peering into my face and I talked to them. I wasn't afraid. They kept me company. The time passed that way."

Winnie refused to acknowledge that anything other than good could come into her life. She faced life free of fear and filled with joy. She knew that right finally resolves everything opposed to it. Though years have passed, her positive outlook on life is still felt in my own.

China Experience

"Even though I walk through the valley of death, I fear not evil, for You are with me."

Psalm 23

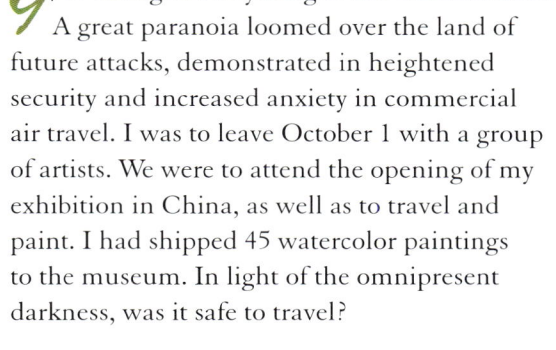

9/11 changed everything in the United States. A great paranoia loomed over the land of future attacks, demonstrated in heightened security and increased anxiety in commercial air travel. I was to leave October 1 with a group of artists. We were to attend the opening of my exhibition in China, as well as to travel and paint. I had shipped 45 watercolor paintings to the museum. In light of the omnipresent darkness, was it safe to travel?

We had to rediscover the omnipresence of God, our sense of protective presence everywhere. Just as the sun warms the atmosphere, so a consciousness of good disables every sign of animosity, disagreement and hateful action. I had been invited by the Chinese government to exhibit my work at the Art Museums of the Forbidden City in Beijing. Some of my fellows traveled, other did not. We were treated royally with a red carpet and banners by the government and the people. Our inordinate loss was acknowledged by their demonstration of welcome, compassion, trust and security.

We left China reassured that good overcomes. Good dissipates everything in opposition to it. We continue to travel free and open which allows good to warm our path just as the sun warns every square inch of the turning Earth.

Turning point.

"Genius is the ability to renew one's emotions in daily experience."
—Paul Cezanne

"Herb plays it better." I thought. He's the family accordion player back home. The man's playing at the café where I sit is jolly and eccentric. Like the bright facades of the buildings here, the music and lights reflect the gaiety of the people in the streets. It works like a duet, like a song sung unto itself.

Plane trees splay light and shadows over the concentric circular patterns of the cobblestones. The dark eyes of discarded shrimp spy the action from their temporary placement around the rims of white porcelain bowls. Warm water of an ancient spa still spills from the 300-year old Mossy Fountain on the Cours Mirabeau, at the corner of Rue de Septemper.

Les Deux Garcons cafe has not changed since Cezanne and other French painters sipped libations, sitting at the same tables Audrey and I now occupy. I am inspired by the same light and textures, in my own way. This is my time to live. I am awed by life itself. It is a new energy.

Time to Move On

"The sanctity of individuality must be maintained if we are to evolve."

—Barkerisms, Page 69

Times and circumstances change and give way from underneath us. This is life and all of us divine creatures do not live according to our designs.

Naturally, just as everything in the universe evolves and goes forward, so relationships change. We go different ways…it is just over…and it is complete. We can spend time in blame or a generation of self-lacerations, or we can bless, release, forgive if necessary, and move on.

Our vision is clouded and every thought is obstructed until we know that God expresses good through every person and every situation.

Chewing on Coca

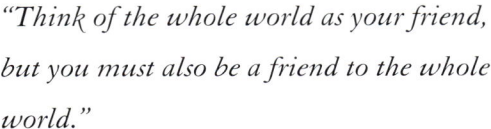

"Think of the whole world as your friend, but you must also be a friend to the whole world."

—Ernest Holmes

Hotel signs in Peru read, "Don't worry, you're not 'doing drugs' if you chew on coca leaves." Hotels regularly give out leaves to tourists. It helps them adjust to life at 12,000 feet. Chewing on coca leaves, I wandered the streets with my art portfolio. I walked slow to feel each cobblestone. I remember every moment of fascination with their architecture and each burst of colorfully embroidered clothing of locals passing by. I stepped aside for a line of llamas. It was like time no longer existed.

Occasionally, I would stop to paint a watercolor. I took a break in the chapel of the Convento de Santo Domingo where I sketched their 18K gold altar. Suddenly, the weight of my gear and the unevenness on my feet brought me to my knees. Was it the coca? Was it the altitude?

Fortunately, a kind gentleman rescued me. He spoke English. He walked me into a nearby hotel and told them, "This lady is lost." I could hardly remember my name, let alone the name of my hotel. The desk man spent twenty minutes phoning every hotel within 10 blocks requesting if they had a Sylvia Miller registered. Once found, the first kind gentleman retrieved his car and drove me the 5 blocks back to my hotel. I offered to compensate him, but he said, "I hope someone will be here for my wife someday."

That is my idea of making friends in a friendly world. I enjoy befriending the world, thinking of the whole world as my friend, and that all the world's forces are supportive of me.

A simple smile~

People ~~share~~ spread love through sharing. A kind word, a simple smile. We can bring positive energy into our lives by smiling, talking more to strangers

"The Man in the Doorway"

To share is to love. A simple smile. A kind word. We bring positive energy into our lives by smiling, by talking more to strangers. Everyone is a stranger on the street.

It was a wet wintry, blistery day, the sort that turns your umbrella inside out. I got out of my car. Along the sidewalk nearby, I noticed a disheveled man curled up in a shallow doorway. He was pressed up against the building's wall in his best attempt to stay out of the elements. As in my nature, I greeted him with a smile and a warm hello.

I walked to the computer shop a half block away and picked up my PC. I stumbled out into the rain loaded with the heavy box and open umbrella. The person that I had just passed a few minutes earlier jumped up and asked if he could help me. He carried my computer to my car. We exchanged a few more kind words and a thank you. I would never have had this lovely connection with this different sort of person had I not stopped to share a gift of a smile. Some relationships with people can be very short, but they can still make a difference. We were strangers once, too.

Morning Coffee

"The material world is but a fleeting shadow of the unseen."

— Myrtle Fillmore

I start my day journaling with coffee and gratitude. What a wonderful way to greet the morning! I pray and affirm abundance of the universe for everyone who is open to its gifts. Material wealth is only part of the prosperous thing gifted. Love and friendship are the truest treasures.

Gratefully, I inherit the copious wealth of the universe. Its Spirit supplies me with abundant happiness and prosperity. Since I know the Source and the Truth, I am not hindered from any Good coming to me. There is no lack of faith, for I trust, therefore I am one with the essence of that faith. All of my hopes, needs and desires are manifested. It is up to me to take care of my needs. Life is my constant supply and source. There is no fear or limitation.

I set my mind into creative motion through my thoughts and activities. None of God's gifts are mine to possess, permanently. They belong to the eternal flow of life. It circulates through gracious giving and receiving. This is the Law of Abundance and for this I am truly grateful.

Morning Mantras

Om mani padme hum, om tare tuttare sohna,
Om mani padme hum, om tare tuttare sohna,
Om mani padme hum, om tare tuttare sohna.

—(an ancient Buddhist mantra)

I slip into my morning prayers, easily. 100 to 108 times, bead to bead, count to count. The Guru bead. Reverse. Repeat, over and over again… A thousand times. A million times. Countless unknown repetitions in tune with the cosmic, rhythms of life. One mala, one rosary bead at a time I quietly slip into my appointed communion with Spirit, with God.

My mind melts into peaceful patterns of silent thoughts. Lovingly, the stress dissipates. I surrender. The powerful, gentle flow of presence washes over me. God dwells within. We are, I am one. From this familiar feeling, my accumulation of gratitude, energy and blessings are now ripe to manifest in my life.

Flow of God through me.

Wholeness

"I praise you, for I am fearfully and wonderfully made. Wonderful are your works; that I know very well."

— Psalm 139:4

God is love. God is wholeness. God is all there is. God is omnipresent, omnipotent and omnipresent. Divine energy flows through within, infusing every cell, tissue and organ with strength and vitality.

Within me are thousands of parts that comprise my whole. My hip is part of the skeleton that frames me. I am a sum part of these parts that allow me to move and feel. There is only one of me and I am a magnificent creation of God.

I have faith in myself, the upcoming replacement hip surgery and my doctors, knowing all is perfect and well. Every cell of my body is bathed in divine light. I give thanks for my body, strength and the amazing way it works and repairs itself. I accept with joy the gift of a new titanium, porcelain hip, know that all is God. I joyfully release this prayer into the Infinite universe knowing that it already is.

Body knows how to heal itself and every cell in my body is bathed in Devine Light

Spiritual energy comes from within as every cell & molecule is. [hip] — it has served me well — it is saying "I am tired and [worn out]." So we are scheduled for [replacement] surgery on Monday, Nov. 19 [at ___]m. at Three Rivers hospital. [It is] where the top of the thigh [meets the soc]ket of the pelvis. The top of the [femur is] like a ball and fits snugly [into the socket] formed by the acetabulum. [The ends] of the hip bones are "slick" [cartilage] cushions and protects the bones [allowing] smooth movement. Ligaments [connect] bones and hold them in place [giving stre]ngth and elasticity too. [The] muscles play an important part

in keeping the joint stable and mobile.

I'm having minimally invasive surgery done, w/ smaller incision from the front or Anterior Approach — 1 small incision on the front of the thigh. I should or definitely will respond quickly because I am whole, healthy and complete. I am a perfect weight, I am active. I am a young 70 year old. I have done my "Leg" exercises. Thank you body for all of these things. I will garden, dance, sing and live life to my fullest with my new hip. It is all one, it is all God and God is good.

acetabulum and shell

femur stem

I see myself as whole and perfect as in pure spirit

femur

Breasts are Beautiful

"Breasts are a scandal because they shatter the border between motherhood and sexuality."

— Iris Marion Young

Breasts are beautiful… All colors, all shapes, one of a pair, all sizes and numbers, those with or without. Breasts are of God Source.

Today I had my yearly mammogram. Any woman will tell you it is an uncomfortable experience. It reminds me of a rather personal and a deeply private journal entry. My awareness of breast issues and the people I love grows every time I view it.

It is a page where I write the names of women in my life that have had or currently live with breast cancer. The list grows longer each year. Some of these women are no longer with us. Most of the names are cancer survivors.

Human Bean Coffee celebrates Breast Awareness Month. As I return to this entry, I am reminded of God Source in the beauty of the breast. Every day I connect with God Source on the page, I remember to celebrate all the breasts, boobs and bosoms of those I hold in memory and in life.

The Dimmer Switch

> "We are God, the power source and the light."
>
> — Rev. Michelle Ingalls

How bright is my life? What would happen if I were to stop in a moment of distress or suffering and look at the truth of my being? I would be creating my next moment with a fresh start.

Subjectively, God is our power source. The energy is a particle gift from God. There is a dimmer switch between us and God. It rates the power supply which becomes the light we find at our center. We control the outcome of the energy through choices, options and spiritual practice. We shift the power away from the storm's center rather than to the storm. Any resistance diminishes the quality of the light.

My center glows bright. I am the source. I believe and trust the power source and the light. If I fail, I must come back to my center. There is no lack. There is no doubt. Any opposition will dim the bulb and the quality of my life. I give 100% to God.

Breaking Down the BRICK WALL to G...

The Brick Wall

"Release the trapped energy that could be doing wonderful things in an un-trapped world." Said Rev. Michelle Ingalls. Get out of your comfort zone. We are part of a grander scheme. It is what I am and who I am. It is my potential.

Often, I forget that. I get so stuck in my comfortable self. This can be a damned solid brick wall. Climb over it. Find a way to circumvent its edges. Concrete and mortar are real stuff to deal with. Will yourself to drive right through the wall.

In life, first we do as the masters do. Then we do as the masters say. Finally, we listen to our own hearts, the Supreme Master. There, the barriers fall away one brick at a time.

Why disturb that feeling of cozy confidence that we know so well? It is there we stop growing. It is then that we become stagnant. Tap into the zone of unlimited potential. Allow it. Enter the zone of enlightenment. Go for the breakthrough! Our heart's desire asks us not to rest against the wall ag...

Make Me Your Instrument

"Lord, make me the instrument of your peace. Where there is hatred, let me show love. Where there is doubt, faith. Where there is despair, hope. Where there is darkness, light. Where there is sadness, joy."

— From the prayer of Saint Frances

I love music. All of it! When I listen to music, it is as if the entire planet's Spirit runs through me like a radio current that harmonizes my soul. It is unseen, but often I see, hear and feel the results. Music is rich storytelling through its vibrational energy of texture, color, tone, form, variation and harmony.

When Rhythm and Blues' Muddy Waters added words to songs previously taboo, meanings of words changed for me. Sounds ranging from Ray Charles to Beyonce are united with pure impassioned soul that play with my heart which sheds any doubt about faith and replaces hatred with love and peace. Country and folk dig deep into my basic American folkloric roots with words of hope, despair and turmoil. Classical, epitomized by Mozart, Beethoven, and Bach, takes my feelings and emotions to a high complex level of sounds that play intricately with my senses and thoughts. Music is life, every bit and piece.

Listen to the colors of your life…heartbeat, boogie your feet in dance tempo, feel the rhythms of your soul, sing your sentimental heart out to the clouds in the sky. Chant, whistle, hum. Sing out of tune with the backyard birds and soon you'll be one of the special symphonic instruments of Spirit. We all have a song that needs to be sung.

Surrender

"To be spiritually minded is life and peace."

— Romans 8:6

I surrender all doubt. I can dream of nothing too great of an undertaking. I surrender to Spirit as I see myself in the eternal flow of change. I open to the restructuring that is a continuous expression of God. I listen to my heart which allows me to walk in the charm of God's love and become part of his greater circle. I question my thoughts and words, but Its reply is to write, again and again. Believe myself. Love myself. Through my journaling and art, I serve.

Infinite intelligence guides me. Feeling, thinking and sensing this All-ness, I enter into a conscious relationship with the divine. In some subtle way, which I cannot explain, Its essence flows out into action. Upon the simplest problems and obstacles in my way, It spills an intelligence and power that is transcendent. Now, I accept the successful action of the divine regulator in everything I do.

Eye of the Storm

"Life is not about waiting for the storm to pass… it's about learning to dance in the rain."

— Vivian Greene

There is an eye, or an "I" in every storm. Like myself, a hurricane's center is its calmest part. The hurricane can become my personal storm. I can let the winds of the storm be my tempest…or I can be the creator of my own life and allow serenity of center to control the uncontrollable. The whole universe has its creation within me. When I control the squalling twists, the disturbances of the winds of the air become still.

With hurt, pain or loss, my life becomes the whirling and twirling around the destructive vortex. The illusions in my mind swirling unchecked become the storm. It vacillates my very verve. It damages my soul when it spins out of control.

I go to my quiet center. I find the safe spot within. I discover the divine, the peace, the comfort. Wherever I go and whatever I do I carry this place of refuge within me. At any moment I can breathe into my heart and feel safe and secure. I can dance amidst any storm.

The eye or "I" of the storm. The Eye is the God Spirit within us. The eternal Mind or Internal Mind does not hold anything against anyone. We can let the winds of the hurricane within us consume us or we can control it, make it our own creation. The entire universe has its creation in us. The hurricane becomes our internal storm. Meditate with "storm" to find the devine. The illusions of your mind can swirl out of control and become the storm. You must go to your center — the storm will pass ~ How you relate to an experience not how it relates to you. Who you are today sets the stage for tomorrow. Your thoughts, beliefs, past, actions are part of the universe. Bondage to the past is inevitable

REV-MARDEE 4/1/02

Primordial Soup

The universe exists in my hand; the loving, age descriptive lines; the pores that breathe and expire; the burnt brown blemishes of the sun kissed surface. I look deeper into my being, to where the abysmal DNA spirals to form my individualized self. Here are the atoms that form the molecular makings of hydrogen, oxygen and carbon. They are the original ingredients of the universal cosmos. This is God source.

My mind travels into the abyss of that primary cradle. It yearns to understand the personal mother, to clutch her soul. It reaches out into the planetary space to awaken that spot where all things originate. It mixes with the ingredients that produce the organic primordial soup. Its comforting nature nourishes, provides and protects. It is the vital food source of life. It is the Oneness of all form.

The same energy may have traveled down through time from the far reaches of the cosmos into the inorganic makings of petroglyphic rocks that define any postcard from Arizona. It may have been reconstituted and mixed into the royal soup of a Russian Tsar. And maybe, just maybe, that broth became me in the mid-twentieth century. Call it ether, matter, light, nature, Spirit. It feels like a dream. It is not, for I am, and God is.

> "What I want is to live of that initial and primordial something that was what made some things reach the point of aspiring to be human."
>
> — Clarice Lispecton

Meditation I Am

I visualize myself, than look deep into my hand, its lines of character, the pores, the blemishes of sun kissed surface — I look deeper into my being, into my cellular makeup, life and spirit, made up of DNA of who I am — molecules of H, O, C, releasing energy released by the charge of neutron and proton all from a single cell source of spirit or fuel — originally coming from the universal cosmos. In the beginning there was only cosmic spirit from which matter sprang together to produce the entire God universe — that exists today And So — I AM, God Is —

January 31, 2012

"*We get stuck in our brew of life.*"

— Reverend Michelle Ingalls

Original Brew

Coffee filter. Coffee grounds. Water, set, brew! Life's brew! What would our brew taste like if a touch of something undesirable got into the grounds? It wouldn't be our ever reliable Starbucks!

Think of the coffee bean as life's original brew. It's perfect. The mind can work like the coffee filter. It removes unsolicited stuff until it gets clogged up. Often, our minds are steeped in unwanted thoughts that end up producing unpleasant results. Creatively, we can learn to identify those undesirable feelings and beliefs to get the best taste out of life.

Fears, guilt and anxieties get in the way of quality. We get stuck. We can't move ahead. Regardless of how much filtering we do, life is still disagreeable. The richness and purity of the taste is affected. It becomes acidic. Meditation and prayer remove unwanted beliefs playing hostage to our taste buds. To satisfy our palate with the best brew possible, we must filter out the bitterness of our mind.

Monkey Matters

We choose to live in the world of Spirit, or get stuck in the world of conditions (of cause & effect.)

> "The more power one gives to one's thoughts, the more completely they believe that their thoughts have power, the more power they will have."
> — Ernest Holmes

SPIRIT/GOD — MAN or WORLDLY CONDITIONS

Love ~ Hate
Good ~ evil
Joy ~ Despair
hope ~ fear

OPPOSITES EXIST ONLY IN Form

Pairs of cause & effect actually complement one another in the physical universe.

in support of conscious evolution

Rev. Ruth Kirby said one Sunday morning, "The chatter that goes on in our heads, goes on forever. These voices take in all. We are only the observer watching the task of the mind at work."

I believe the whole universe lives in my mind. Often, it is filled with chatter, chatter and more chatter. When active, the indwelling voices sound more like a rainforest of mating monkeys than a well-orchestrated chorus of infinite knowledge. One monkey makes me laugh. Another brings me to tears. Somedays, the entire forest is alive, like a monkey choir, out of tune and desperate to be heard.

These days are a gift. They remind me to look around at the good in my life and listen with gratitude in my heart. It is from this place that my story comes alive in the way I choose.

67

Love that Sticks...

What is my prayer hidden inside for God to answer?

I share a delight as one seagull feather sails in the brilliance of sunshine and gliding down settles on glittering sand, a moment beyond anything I or the feather could have ever imagined…a moment beyond imagination.

It is a very intimate connection with God and my angelic spirits. My energy dreamingly becomes the feather as driftwood and raffia-like seaweed come together to send thoughts and prayers into the omnipresent universe. Bound between these natural layers, a sacred secret prayer written on paper, is passed into Spirit's hands with thoughts and words of the deepest gracious intention.

"In centering prayer, the sacred word is not the object of attention, but rather, the expression of the intention of the will."

— Thomas Keating

What is my prayer hidden inside for only God to answer. I surrender to the presence and power of God within me!

Paper Dolls

"God's presence fills each heart in our Nation with peace and love, including me."

— Reverend Michelle Ingalls

I cried. I mourned. I felt profound shock. Now numb, I asked, "Why the young, carefree, innocent, seven and eight-year-olds?"

Maybe by writing and cutting out paper dolls, one for each young soul, I can grip onto some kind of understanding. Anything that will replace the shock, the anger, and the grief. Each shape I cut out brings more sobs, and more tears that dampen the paper. I write each name, with the hope it might breathe energy into the inert silhouettes, a spark of life into the shapes…reconnection to their now missing souls.

There is something comforting about the repetitive process. Slow repeated cutting of rounded edges soothes the sharp angles of my insides. I feel an essence of loving energy merge with each cut. Safely, I paste them in my journal until they find their eternal spirits.

We often wonder how we can go on living, how we can go on with our daily lives. We must strengthen our resilience, pad our spiritual bank accounts, so we can continue in the face of adversity. Talk about it. Go-all-out for a balance in our lives. Remind ourselves of people and events that are productive and reassuring. Honor our feelings. Do something meaningful. So, I cut paper dolls.

Red Dance Shoes

Secretly, I dream of owning a pair of red dancing shoes – ruby red shoes that urge me to tango and rhumba romantically to the rhythms of life. I could pray for them, but it is absolutely silly for me to think of asking God for those red shoes, specifically. I know that God doesn't sit around, at my beck and call, sorting through and moving shoe boxes around in order to fill orders in my life. How do I get the things I covet?

I embrace the idea that there is abundance in the universe and I deserve to have it. I develop an unwavering, steadfast faith in what I desire out of life and go for it. I dare to conceive that I am worthy of those shoes and so, much, much more. Faith is knowing that I am surrounded by infinite possibility and it passes into expression through me when I ask and allow it to happen. I graciously pray, knowing that all of the copious wealth that life offers are mine to own, including those damned red dance shoes!

I dare dream of things greater than myself.

Failure is impossible with the universe working with me.

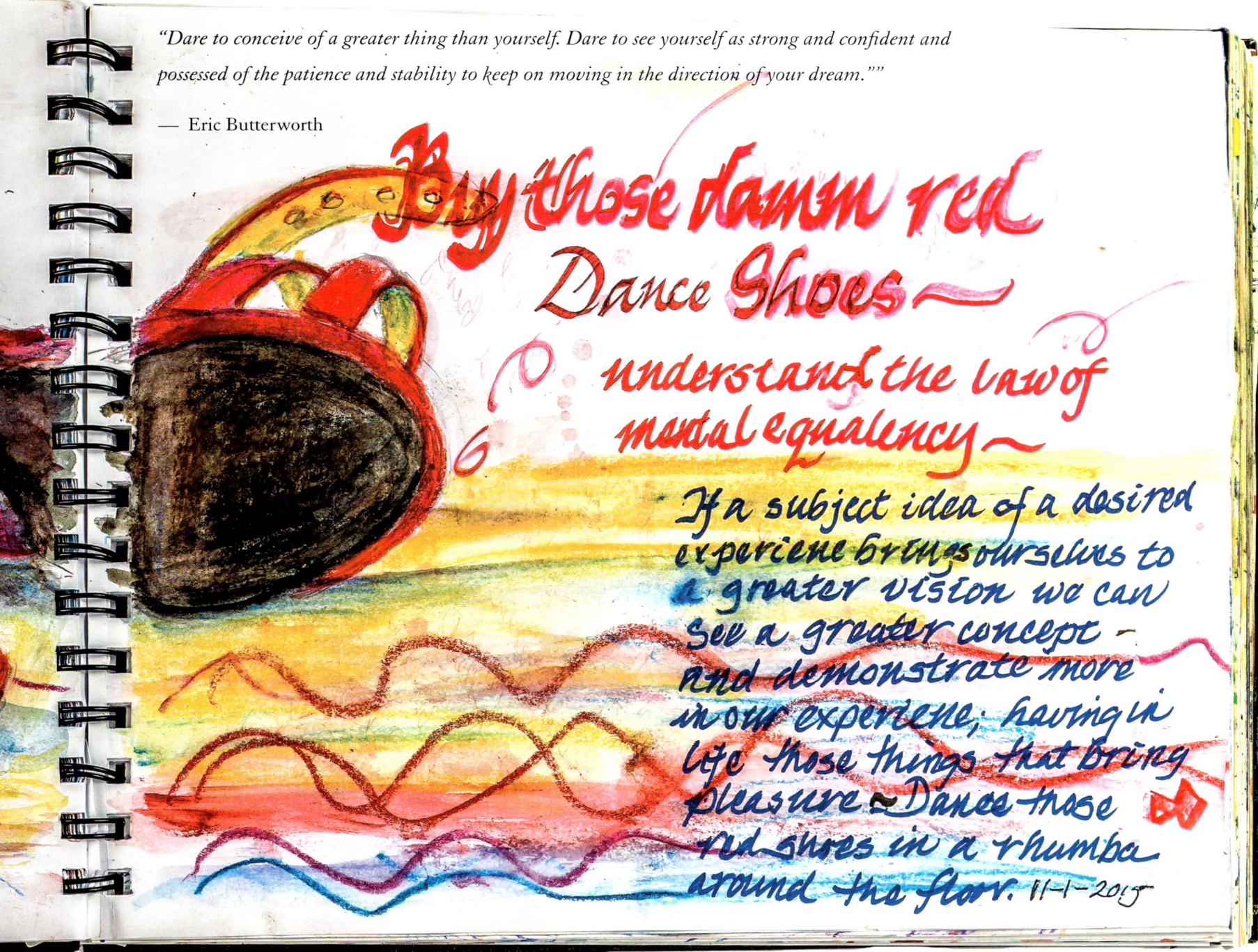

"Dare to conceive of a greater thing than yourself. Dare to see yourself as strong and confident and possessed of the patience and stability to keep on moving in the direction of your dream.""
— Eric Butterworth

Buy those damn red Dance Shoes ~

understand the law of mental equalency ~

If a subject idea of a desired experience brings ourselves to a greater vision we can see a greater concept ~ and demonstrate more in our experience; having in life those things that bring pleasure ~ Dance those red shoes in a rhumba around the floor. 11-1-2015

Next o'Kin

"You can choose your friends but you sho' can't choose your family, an' they're kin to you no matter, whether you acknowledge it or not, and it makes you look silly when you don't."

— Harper Lee,
 "To Kill a Mockingbird"

Death always brings us closer. Beneath the surface we are more than the tags and limitations we have labeled upon us. Tony's labels describe his life…cub scout, railroad gangbuster, Misfit motorcycle gang member, Linda's soulmate, and Pentecostal Church congregant.

They poured out of the woodwork to celebrate his life. Tony had three children he claimed, two or three more that claimed him, and a few other "adopted kids." Who were blood relatives? Who claimed to be? It doesn't really matter. The "relatives" all said the same things, "Tony was loving and compassionate." There were those covered with body piercing, others with gang tattoos, a few ragged ruffians and many "normal" professional folks. We are all salt and peppered, a mixed bag of colors, a pleasant incongruent mix of souls. His "celebration" reminded me, once again, to be proud to be an Emmert. Thank you, brother.

Let us choose to treat others as children of the Divine, united, if not by DNA, by our spiritual lineages. We are all rooted in pure spirit and oneness. We are all next o'kin.

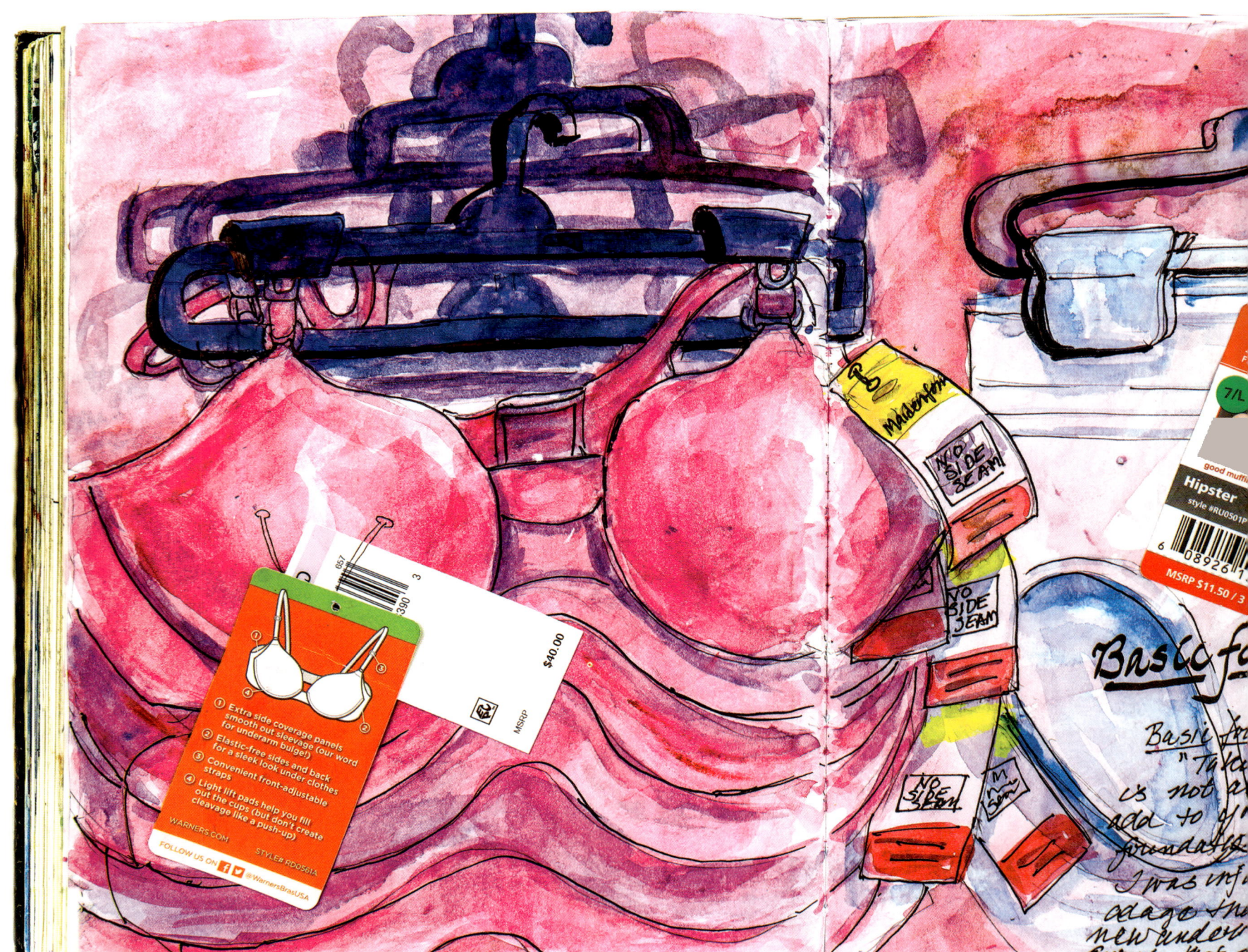

Basic Foundation

"Taking care of yourself is not another extra thing to add to your to-do list, it is the foundation of life."

— Sarah Yost

While I prepared for a trip, I remembered the old adage, "always wear clean underwear. God forbid something unforeseen happens and we are found with the dreaded, dirty, tattered underwear."

Cy and I headed for Macy's. I went to the women's lingerie and he to the men's. Among the ladies' racks, I had to squat down as my size was on the bottom. Suddenly, while down on my haunches, I realized I could not move! Without a salesperson in sight, I reached into my purse, grabbed my cell phone and shouted to Cy, "I need help! I'm stuck by the bras!"

Beneath the D's I saw his shoes. "Down here," I called. He stopped. Quickly, I reached up. I grabbed one of the support bars. Much like the underwire that's lost its lift, I grabbed the support rack which rained down an entire wall's worth of bras and panties. I was humiliated.

Cy laughed out loud. He helped me to my feet. Piece by piece, we put the display back up. As we exited the store, I thought, "How could I let myself go?" From that moment on, my healthy body became "my foundation of life."

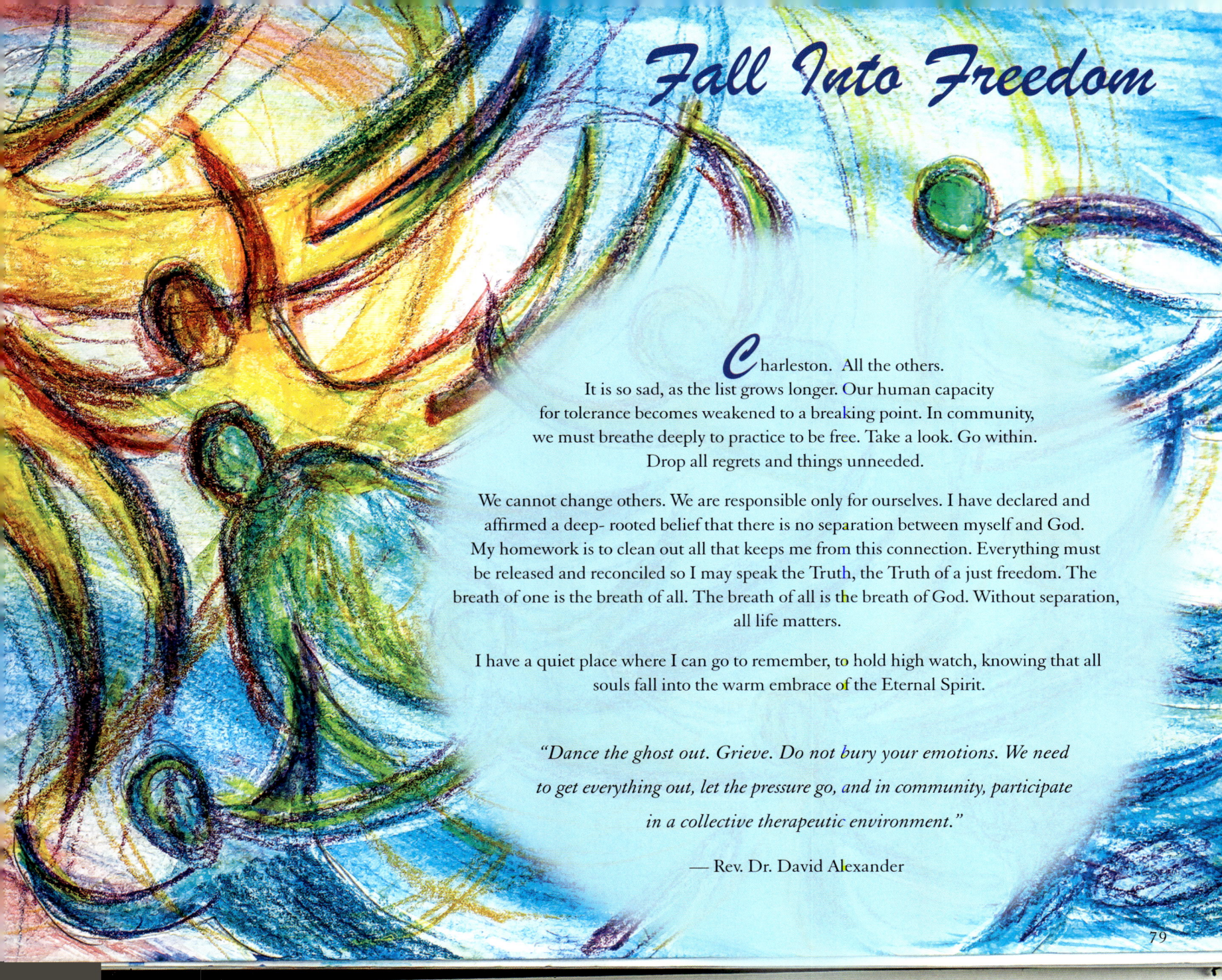

Fall Into Freedom

Charleston. All the others.
It is so sad, as the list grows longer. Our human capacity for tolerance becomes weakened to a breaking point. In community, we must breathe deeply to practice to be free. Take a look. Go within. Drop all regrets and things unneeded.

We cannot change others. We are responsible only for ourselves. I have declared and affirmed a deep-rooted belief that there is no separation between myself and God. My homework is to clean out all that keeps me from this connection. Everything must be released and reconciled so I may speak the Truth, the Truth of a just freedom. The breath of one is the breath of all. The breath of all is the breath of God. Without separation, all life matters.

I have a quiet place where I can go to remember, to hold high watch, knowing that all souls fall into the warm embrace of the Eternal Spirit.

"Dance the ghost out. Grieve. Do not bury your emotions. We need to get everything out, let the pressure go, and in community, participate in a collective therapeutic environment."

— Rev. Dr. David Alexander

Love Beyond Boundaries

"Love is love, and it flows through all."

— Patrick Soran

It is difficult to describe, love. Love exists as what is sensed and what is seen. Love is to be desired. Love transcends all genders and labels. Emotionally, it leaves you giddy. It hits you in the gut and nothing makes sense. Love exists even for my 97-year-old Aunt Mary.

Still a striking grand dame at her age, Aunt Mary fell head-over-heels in love with her young, handsome, Greek caregiver. Seriously, she talked about marrying him! During one of our telephone conversations we talked about love, different types of love; the deep profound love she had for her late husband of 54 years; the hug-me type of love she gave her children. I told her that it was okay to love this young man; it was a special kind of caring friendship. It was poetic. She gave herself permission to enjoy his poetry. Her desperate loneliness slipped away.

We are all going to die. Ask yourself how do you want to spend your life? Love is all about loving ourselves and loving others. Love is beyond boundaries. We are all worthy of knowing love: old, young? Black, White? Straight, Gay? It doesn't matter! Love is love, no matter.

"Team Rowing"

"What is the spiritual value of rowing? The losing of self entirely to the cooperative effort of the crew as a whole."

— George Yoeman Pocook

Rowing on the Williamette River, Portland, Oregon

I am mesmerized. The rowing teams are out for their spring drilling on the Willamette River. They are regular people, like our neighbors next door, who row as a family. It is a beautiful sight to watch, as oars cut clean and rhythmically through the water's surface.

I recall several paintings by Thomas Eakins, one that I saw in the National Gallery of London of rowers, of fit men and women. It's a sport where muscle alone is not enough; hearts and minds must also be one. In "The Boys in the Boat," Daniel J. Brown wrote, "The sport calls for knowing that when one's everyday strength is depleted you can draw on a mysterious energy of a far greater power."

It is like a community that pulls together to witness a perfect harmony where everything is right. The values can extend to the greater world. If we synchronize our efforts and energies with the natural unfolding of God's universe, we can all row through life without conflict, together in peace and harmony.

Memorial Day Sunday

Earth is Crammed with... Little Bit of H... from...

Sunday - May 27, 2012

Ruth Miller - Joy is the unfallible sign of heaven. When you feel joy you feel heaven. As something falls apart something else is taking its place. The planet is not separate from heaven. One presence, one power is <u>omnipresent</u>, unlimited life, love, joy, abundance are here in one place. Every thing is at hand to use now. All power is delivered unto me, is present now. We have been told it isn't - to overcome this we can do Affirmations. Choose what you know is true - say and affirm it over, over and over again. <u>Earth is crammed with Heaven</u>. When you look at beauty from the inside out your perspective changes. The world comes around. The more beauty you

... on the more you got on earth. What we focus on i... It is not crammed with fear a... You can bring heaven closer... reality. <u>Morphogenetic</u> pow... of groups intentions. What i... you between you and heav... Everything you needed was t... moment and every single sp... fully at hand. There is an inf... for every moment, fresh air... people at the moment. Cultu... with an appreciation of who... appreciate our bodies, and c... are. The "I can't" <u>keeps</u> me in... and our lives begin to ...
We make a shift in appreciat...

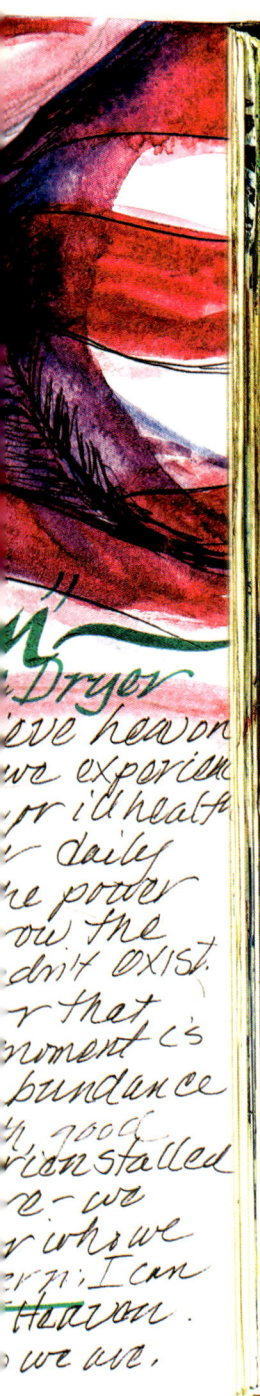

A Little Bit of Heaven

"Earth is crammed with a little bit of heaven."

— Reverend Dr. Ruth L. Miller

Our universe, our planet, our country and even the streets are all infallible signs of heaven. Our planet is not separate from heaven. We own it. The American dream is available every moment, in every place because of this omnipresence. Our Declaration of Independence guarantees this heavenly fulfillment for all people with the phrase, "life, liberty and the pursuit of happiness."

I know two families who are part of the American dream workforce. They are happy, contented, industrious families with strong values and work ethics. They are fulfilling their visions by creating a future of choice. Their children are graduating from colleges and universities. Leticia, Efren and Fermin are Latino immigrants who clean my house and work in my garden. I consider them to be among my friends.

They are making a difference not only in their own lives but also their community. They came here impoverished but not without culture and ideals. We teach and learn from each other. Our country has flourished because it is nourished by so many sources, cultures and people. Each one helps create an earth that is "crammed with a little bit more of heaven."

Pearls of Wisdom

Pearls form when the proverbial grain of sand works its way into an oyster. In defense from the particle, the oyster releases a fluid of nacre to coat the irritant. Layer upon layer is deposited until a lustrous, highly prized pearl forms. Once a symbol of power and wealth, pearls were coveted by strong independent women like Cleopatra and Jacqueline Kennedy Onassis.

Sometimes, women have stories of tragedy and trauma. Like an oyster, they sit clamped and closed due to their loss of beauty and essence. If only they were to remember the pearl! Every time a woman remembers her pearl, she taps into the power that breaks the chain of her limiting belief patterns. Each instance of women empowering each other past societal and religious conditioning agitates another layer of luminous beauty to each other's core.

The loss of our precious essence is the loss of the expression that God made us to be. To rediscover the power that resides within is to reawaken the pearls of wisdom that will return luster and light to our lives. Jackie's famous, triple stranded pearl necklace was made of glass. Barbara Bush wore them too. It was how they wore them that brought their light to life.

Paper Cranes

"*I will write peace on your wings and you will fly all over the world.*"

— Sadako Sasaki

Thousands of origami cranes hang from the rafters of the sanctuary. It is said that 1,000 folded cranes make dreams come true. It is as if they hold high watch over the service. "Who folded all of these?" I think Alison knows.

A crane is thought to be a symbol of good fortune, longevity and peace. After WWII, a young girl named Sadako Sasaki was diagnosed with leukemia. She was from Hiroshima. Sadako was determined to fold 1,000 cranes in hope of world peace. She only completed 645 before she died. Her classmates folded the remaining 365 in her honor.

It takes only the amount of time to fold one paper crane to find a presence of personal peace. It is a meditative gesture that makes the dream of peace in the world come true, one crease of origami at a time. I just folded mine. Have you folded yours?

Black Dots

This sermon reminded me of a Max Lucado fable where the peasants were branded with stars of praise or dots of shame. At one time or another, we all feel the weight of dots placed upon us. My dots include being forced to write with my right hand and being picked last at kickball because I was too awkward when it came my turn up to the plate.

I care for a loved one buried beneath a mound of dots. He is a creative, intelligent, sensitive person who is both mentally and physically disabled. His mound began to grow at an early age. Fixed in the dense dotted darkness, the tracks of his mind twist inside out and upside down. Life becomes a rollercoaster ride. Often, he cries out in pain. Often, in silence. If I hold his hand long enough, a different person emerges from beneath the suffocating mass.

It is here I feel free from the weight of my dots.

"Be a watch dog; an observer; a listener; a person that cares. Sometimes, that is all it takes. We can all become care-givers, making a difference by allowing those that are different to shed one dot at a time."

— Reverend Barbara Wuest

Indwelling Spirit

Ernest Holmes wrote: "The indwelling Spirit alone maintains the identity."

Art is the essence of my life. I choose to seek the repository of my heart. My sketch book is my journal. Quietly, I sit in the space of my heart. Then, I allow the ideas to flow onto the page like the blood that courses through the four chambers of my heart. This union of body and page awaken the slumbering fibers of paper within my soul.

My truth of life dwells within my heart. I am afraid that without God in my heart, I would not know this truth. With this in heart, I embrace the gratitude of how my life is unfolding now that Leukemia inhabits my body.

I accept the deep awareness that I am to voice to others. As others are touched by my work on the page, I realize, I am immortal. My essence of life and the sacred space of my heart are what color my idea of Love. I did not choose Leukemia. Yet, every day is a choice to choose God. It is here I know love.

One God, Many Paths

"May I be well, may I be secure, may I be happy.
May you be well, may you be secure, may you be happy.
May all being be well, may all beings be secure, may all beings be happy."

— New Thought Meditation

The Yogananda memorial in Delhi is a quiet interval of solitude. It exists within walls that separate a tranquil setting from the chaos of a city of over 16 million people.

The tree canopy scatters light across the stone pathway. It is a peaceful walk through this lovely garden. I found it a special place for writing and contemplation.

Along the winding walk, sculptural forms depict quotes and symbols of a dozen or so of the major religions of the world, all embracing inclusivity in a universe that works for all. One read, "Calm, Joy and Freedom."

"Finally, all of you have a unity with Spirit, sympathy, love for one another, a tender heart and a humble mind."

— 1 Peter 3:8

Learning Patience

It is an arduous, fourteen-hour bus ride through the Himalayan foothills to visit Babaji's Cave. We sit packed, shoulder to shoulder. The bus tosses my face to the window. Cavernous ravines plunge straight down to the Ganges. Oddly, it reminds me of Hellgate Canyon in Southern Oregon. Each passing minute wrenches another knot in my gut. A whisper from my childhood echoes, "Patience is a virtue."

I am patient with myself and with the others and with the driver who seems to hit every rock on the winding road. To quell the painful sense that we are about to plunge to our deaths, my eyes focus on the minutiae of the landscape. I pull out my sketch pad and draw.

The rocky movement keeps my drawing loose, a look I like. It is as if Spirit has taken my hand to guide the pencil's tip across the page. I feel a special presence. Before I know it, the drawing lies complete and we stand alive at our final destination. Once again, I am reminded that being patient is a way of making peace with what is out of my control, a way of letting go.

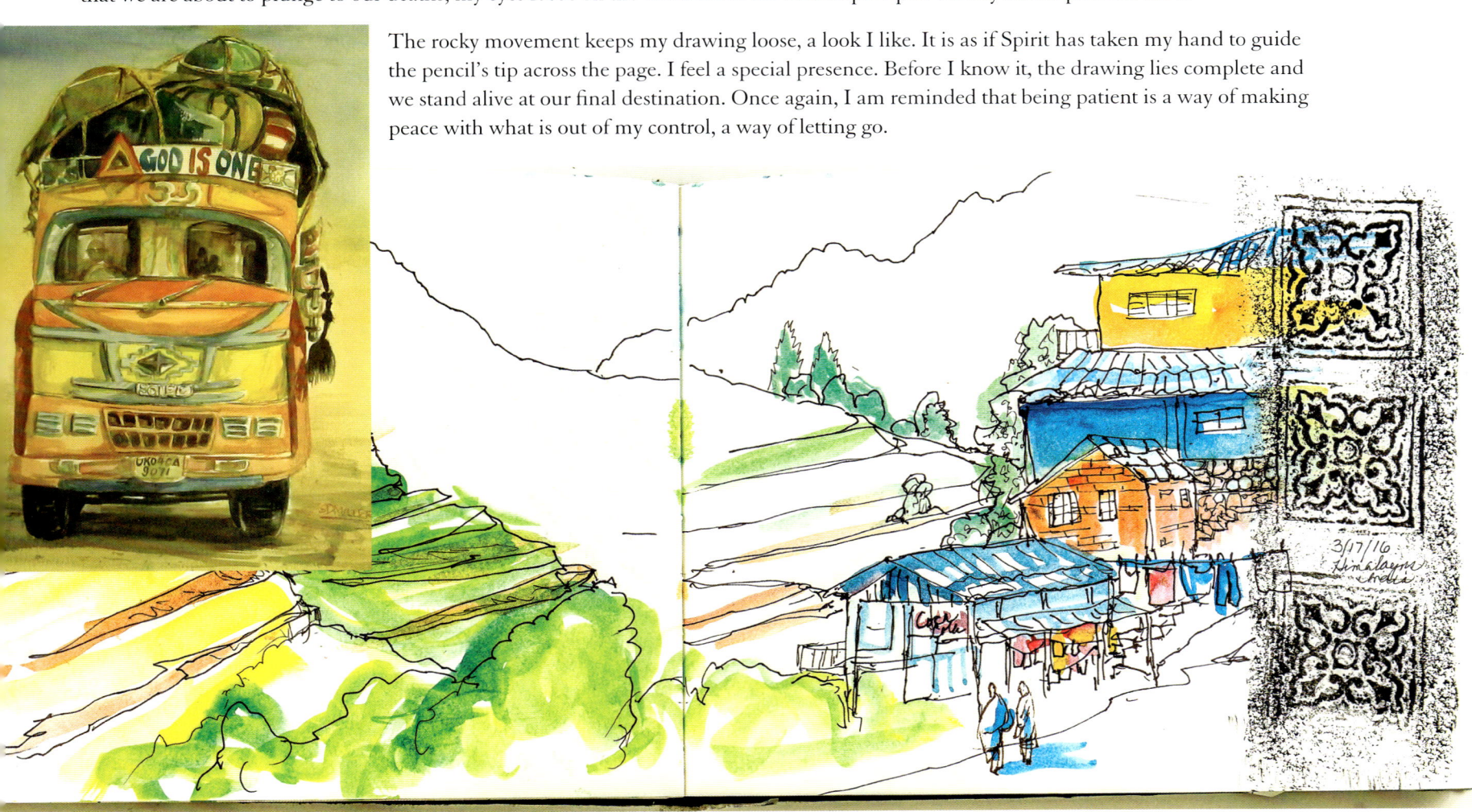

Varanasi Gnats

Today was significant for me. Pilgrims come to the gnats, the steps that line the banks of the River Ganges. It is here they wash away their sins in the sacred waters. They come to cremate their loved ones. The most intimate rituals of life and death take place in public. I couldn't turn away.

The sights, sounds and smells I experienced on the gnats were overwhelming and intoxicating. I was carried away by the wafts of incense and the feeling of well-worn temple floors beneath my feet.

Cows passed me going down the steps to graze on fresh funeral flowers. The untouchables attended the funeral fires. I came to look, but I too, was caught up by it all. My state of consciousness was altered. From a place deep within I felt that a friend of mine had made his transition.

It was confirmed with a 3:00 AM phone call from home that morning. I was okay. I had already celebrated his passing.

Varanasi
3/18 – 3/21/2016

" 'I am not the doer of the action,' says Krishna, as a union with the Divine is met. 'Our senses are things interacting with other form: eyes see, ears hear, noses smell. All is form.'"
— The Bhagavad Gita

Miracles

What stirs my soul? What will I regret at the end? What lives on after we die? I believe each moment of life is sacred. Life is a miracle. It is the pure energy of love. We live within the omnipresence of God's energy, as a microbe or human. Thus we witness life in every moment. We are one with the flow of life.

I accept and surrender, in complete faith, that all exists in God. I am an individualization of this Oneness. I am here for some very special reason. God inspires me to discover His secrets. I create small everyday miracles or grand, life-changing ones. When we see ourselves no different than the sky, the water and the earth, we become one with the Universal source.

This is God consciousness. It enables a comforting emergence of a loving, peaceful energy that flows unimpeded, undisturbed. God works miracles through me. God stirs my soul. I am a vessel through which we co-create. I allow God's warmth to wash over me. I soak it up. I let miracles happen. I let God happen. I have no regrets.

Gratitude List

I am graciously grateful for the following people and their generous help, support and influences in producing this book. With them, it happened.

It is abundantly clear to me that all the people on this list, deserve my utter thanks and profound sincerity. I was especially charmed by my editor, Vincent, who pursued the book with focus and respect. At first I had free rein, as I sorted out what I wanted to say and how I would say it. Then, he rolled up his sleeves and weighed in with such in-depth perspectives and words, that I became a student and a writer. I absolutely enjoyed Deborah, my talented and creative publisher, who allowed me to become an intimate part of the book's layout and design. Ray, my gifted photographer, spent many hours producing beautiful images of the pages from my sketchbooks, capturing the minute details, such as the textural fibers of the paper and true color. It was a worthy journey; the finished book, our creation, from the inside out.

Editor – Vincent Eggleston, CA

Photographe – Raymond Lawrence, OR

Publisher – Deborah Perdue, Illumination Graphics and Applegate Valley Publishing, OR.

Proofreader – Dr. Irene Thomas Howard, Santa Fe, NM
Supportive and helpful people – Cy Le Gare, Claire Sierra, Georgena Eggleston

My family – mother, Margaret Emmert; sisters, Barbara Roberts and Vicky Galberth; brothers, Anthony and Wiley Emmert; Aunt Mary; Aunt Winnie; Herbert Miller, and Aunt Vi.

My Friends – Beth, Julan, Wanda, Audrey, George, Barbara and Gil, Mary, Judy, Laura and Lois.

All my current and past students.

Influential People and Teachers

Ernest Holmes – founder of Religious Science, part of Science of Mind and the New Thought movement

Reverend Michelle Ingalls – Minister at Grants Pass Center for Spiritual Living, Grants Pass OR, and Senior Minister One Heart One Mind Center for Spiritual Living, San Diego

Reverend Dr. David Alexander – Senior Minister at New Thought Center for Spiritual Living, Lake Oswego, OR

Reverend Dr. Ruth L. Miller – Minister and author, including *150 Years of Healing and Hidden Power*; *Make the World Go Away* and *Mary's Power*

Reverend Ruth Kirby

Reverend Barbara Wuest – Minister at New Thought Center for Spiritual Living, Lake Oswego, OR

Alison Hilber – LSP, Center for Spiritual Living, Lake Oswego, OR, author of *I Am Who I AM…Sacredly Accepting my Body*

Lois Benson – author of *Joy in Small Pieces* Year 72nd, *It's the Journey – Living it Well* and *A Journal in Poetry*, the 70th Year

Philip Goldberg – author of *American Veda: From Emerson to the Beatles to Yoga and Meditation*, *How Indian Spirituality Changes the West*

Influential Books and Magazines

The Science of Mind a textbook written by Ernest Holmes

The Science of Mind Magazine

The Daily Word magazine

Siddhartha by Herman Hesse

A Mid-Summer's Night's Dream by William Shakespeare

The Boys in a Boat by Daniel James Brown

The Upanishads, a translation by Eknath Easwaren

The Bahagavad Gita, a translation by Eknath Easwaren

Spiritual Economics by Eric Butterworth

The American Veda by Phil Goldberg

Autobiography of a Yogi by Paramhansa Yogananda

Material Resources

Circle Stickers

Dutch Door Press- Labels and Stickers

Studio Calico Collections

Hearts for Love-stickers and window stickers

Stampendous-stickers

Dover Publications-stickers and transfers

About the Author

Sylvia Miller is a professional teacher, published writer, and award winning artist. She holds Bachelor's Degrees in Art and Biological Sciences, California Standard Life Teaching Credentials and is a Certified Spiritual Practitioner with the Centers for Spiritual Living. She is best known for her spontaneous watercolor paintings. She taught art and science in California secondary schools for 30 years. As a second career, she teaches watercolor and artistic journaling workshops, both domestically and internationally. Her art articles have appeared in *American Artist* and *Watercolor Magazine*, Daler & Rowney's *The Art Paper*, and other publications. She is constantly evolving in her life and unfolding her purpose. She has always had the desire to express her heart's voice on the sketchbook page. In the process of filling countless journal pages, she discovered she is a writer. Her writing and drawings beautifully merge together as she continues to spiritually grow and expand. Her goal is to be of loving service to the Universe. She graciously shares Spirit's special gifts that flow through her, with you. She lovingly bares her heart and soul completely…from the inside out.

Sylvia Miller

Sylvia D. Miller

www.sylviamillerwatercolor.com

sylviamiller541@gmail.com

Notes

Notes